Ellie and the Clown Crisis

HEATHER BUTLER

ILLUSTRATED BY
JOEL BUCKLEY

Scripture Union, 207-209 Queensway, Bletchley, Milton Keynes,
MK2 2EB, England
Email: info@scriptureunion.org.uk
Website: www.scriptureunion.org.uk

Scripture Union Australia, Locked Bag 2, Central Coast Business Centre,
NSW 2252
Website: www.su.org.au

Scripture Union USA, PO Box 987, Valley Forge, PA 19482
Website: www.scriptureunion.org

British Library Cataloguing-in-Publication Data.

A catalogue record of this book is available from the British Library.

Printed and bound in Great Britain by Creative Print and Design (Wales) Ebbw Vale.

Cover design: kwgraphicdesign

↳ Scripture Union is an international Christian charity working with churches
in more than 130 countries, providing resources to bring the good news about
Jesus Christ to children, young people and families and to encourage them to
develop spiritually through the Bible and prayer.

As well as our network of volunteers, staff and associates who run holidays,
church-based events and school Christian groups, we produce a wide range of
publications and support those who use our resources through training
programmes.

CONTENTS

For Cin. H.B.

For Nikki and Lily May. J.B.

MUM WANTS TO BE A CLOWN

Before this story began there was Joseph, his mum and dad, and all his brothers. We know about them because they're in the Bible.

Meanwhile, 3,800 years later, in 42 Milton Road…

Bert was there, as usual. Ellie needed him tonight.

If ELLIE'S MUM AND DAD ARGUE MUCH MORE THEY'LL EXPLODE.

After a while the shouting stopped and all they could hear was the television.

Ages later Mum and Dad tiptoed up the stairs. They thought Ellie was asleep, but she wasn't.

"Your mother wants to learn how to become a clown," Dad said, as he crunched his way through a piece of toast the next morning. "There's a course in Brighton she wants to go on. It'll cost an arm and a leg but she doesn't care."

Mum turned on him.

"I've told you, I'll pay for it myself. I'm going to find a job today so it won't cost you anything."

Dad's chair scraped across the floor as he stood up.

"I'm going to work," he snapped. "One of us has to do something sensible."

Ellie stared down at her cereal bowl. It stared back up at her but didn't say anything. Neither did Mum.

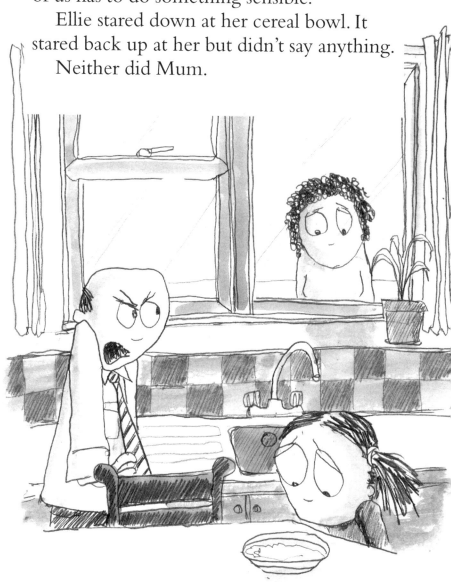

On her way to school Ellie called for Toni. They talked about which races Mike would enter them for in their Swimming Club Gala. If their times were fast enough they would go through to the county finals!

"I hope he puts me in for backstroke," Ellie said. "That's my fastest stroke and I bet you'll have to race against Polly."

"You reckon?"

"You're better than she is now."

"You reckon?"

"I do."

Polly was taller than anyone else,
and a show off
and a bully
and she had
beautiful long hair
and long
eyelashes.

Her best
stroke was
freestyle.
So was Toni's.

When Jacob's son, Joseph, was 17 years old, he took care of the sheep with his 11 brothers. Jacob loved Joseph more than he did his other sons and gave him a fine coat to show that he was his favourite son. Joseph's brothers hated him and would not be friendly to him.

One day Joseph had a dream. "Listen to what I dreamt," he told his brothers. "The sun, the moon and 11 stars bowed down to me."

JOSEPH'S BROTHERS WON'T LIKE THAT ANY MORE THAN ELLIE LIKES POLLY SHOWING OFF.

13

That day at school Mrs Jenkins, their
teacher, had cut her finger so she couldn't
write on the white board.

In maths Kevin Harrison had a nosebleed

and at lunch time Jerome Portsworth was sick, just as Ellie bit into a tuna sandwich.

Apart from that, it was an ordinary day.

In the evening Mum drove Ellie to the swimming pool. She had applied for a job at the book shop in town.

"If I get the job, you'll have to let yourself in the house, after school," Mum said. "Would you mind?"

Ellie thought about it.

Gregory would be there.

So would the fridge and the television and it would only be for an hour.

"I'd be all right," she said, which made Mum sigh and smile at the same time.

Ellie looked at her.

Mum loved making people laugh and did daft things like pulling faces at children sitting in supermarket trolleys and juggling baked bean tins in the kitchen. She'd make a good clown.

SWIMMING AND WHOPPER TOPPERS

"In the girls' 100 metres freestyle will be Angela, Polly, Cindy, Toni, Dianna and Sasha," Mike said.

"And don't think you're going to win, you four-eyed crab," Polly hissed at Toni. Toni ignored her.

"She's worried!" Ellie hissed in Toni's other ear.

"You reckon?" Toni whispered back.

They both giggled, the sort of nervous giggle you make when you're a bit scared of someone.

Joseph's brothers were jealous of him, and they hated him more and more. One day they made plans to kill him.

"Look, here comes the hero of those dreams!" they said. They pulled off his fine coat and threw him into a dry well. When some merchants* came by, Joseph's brothers took him out of the well, and for 20 pieces of silver they sold him.

*A merchant buys and sells things. Or is it an ant called Merch?

... AND THAT'S HOW HE ENDED UP IN EGYPT. BET HE WAS SCARED WHEN HIS BROTHERS WERE BEING NASTY TO HIM.

Mike did not want Ellie to race in the backstroke but the 50 metres butterfly. At first she was disappointed.

"You've got good upper body strength and a kick like a

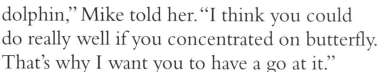

dolphin," Mike told her. "I think you could do really well if you concentrated on butterfly. That's why I want you to have a go at it."

Maybe he was right. Whatever, she would do her best.

It was Dad who picked Ellie up from swimming.

"Your mother has gone late night shopping," he said. "She wants to buy a new dress for when she gets a job. She's in a funny mood at the moment. Did you know she's thinking of buying a unicycle?"

Now that was something to think about.

"I'm too tired to cook. Shall we go to Percy's Pizza Place?"

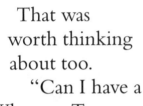

That was worth thinking about too.

"Can I have a Whopper Topper and a Choc Chopper afterwards?"

"Are you sure you can eat all that?" Dad asked.

Sometimes grown-ups ask such silly questions!

CHAPTER 3

THEY'RE STILL ARGUING

Ellie went to Percy's Pizza Place three weeks later as well, this time to celebrate Mum's new job at the book shop. Dad was going to come but had to work late.

"Listen to this," Mum said, between sips of her Diet Coke. She whispered something that made Ellie's eyes nearly pop out of their sockets.

"You're not!"

"I am."

Mum had a wicked grin on her face.
When Ellie came home from school the
next day, Mum's hair was bright red and
green.

"What's Dad going to say?" Ellie gasped.
She found out four hours later.
"If I wanted to live with a
bottle of tomato ketchup
with green stripes
running down its
side," he shouted,
"I'd have gone to
the supermarket
and bought one.
It'd be cheaper!"

"Mum and Dad used to love each other," Ellie told Bert that evening, "but I'm not sure they do anymore."

Bert said nothing of course. He never did.

Polly, meanwhile, was getting worse. She now had a bag with 'World's Greatest Swimmer' written on the side.

"That's what I'm going to be!" she told everyone.

"You reckon?" Toni said.

"Yes I do, and you're stupid because all you ever say is 'you reckon'."

"You reckon?"

Toni did say it a lot, but no one else seemed to mind.

"And you can shut up as well, Ellie Jackson. Don't think you're going to win the butterfly race. You're like an elephant in a life jacket when you swim."

"Ignore her!" Toni said loudly, which is what Ellie did, but it was still not very nice.

Fortunately Polly was in a different class from Toni and Ellie.

So she missed Mrs Jenkins catching flu and the supply teacher's toupee slipping over his eyes when Kevin Harrison

had another nosebleed (this time in geography).

She didn't see Toni's new pen that changed colour when she wrote with it either.

Or Ellie's face when Mum gave her tuna sandwiches for the eighth day running. Mum thought tuna sandwiches would help Ellie swim better!

Just before half term Dad had to go away with work. He had been away before, but not while Mum was working.

"It's only for one night," he shouted when Mum said she didn't want him to go.

"But who's going to walk Gregory?" Mum yelled back.
"You can."
"But I'm too busy."

They were off, going on and on and on at each other.

Ellie crept up to her bedroom and hid under the quilt.

"I don't like it," she whispered to Bert. "They're shouting at each other again and Polly's being horrid and I might come last in the swimming because I've got to do butterfly and Mum's too busy now she's at the shop and…"

Potiphar's wife waited until her husband came home one day.
"That slave of yours tried to get me but I screamed for help and he left his coat and ran out of the house," she told him. Potiphar became very angry and threw Joseph into prison.

YOU WERE RIGHT ABOUT HER NOT LIKING IT!

POOR JOSEPH. HE WOULDN'T HAVE A QUILT TO HIDE UNDER EITHER OR BERT TO TALK TO.

CHAPTER 4
POLLY

"When's the Gala?" Dad asked Ellie the next morning.

"The fifth of April," Mum chipped in. "I've written it on the calendar."

"Must make sure it's in my diary as well," Dad smiled. "I'm not going to miss watching our Ellie show all the others how to win a race!" Ellie grinned. Dad was funny as well, sometimes!

"Are you home at the normal time?" Mum asked him.

"Think so."

"See you then. Have a good day."

Dad leaned over and kissed Mum on the cheek.

Ellie smiled inside. Mum and Dad were friends.

Today would be a good day.

It was as well.

The maths test wasn't too hard and at play time Toni fell over and hurt her knee.

That wasn't good but when Mrs Jenkins let them stay in the library at lunch time because of it, that was good. They giggled at page 57 of Kevin's favourite book.

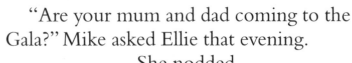

"Are your mum and dad coming to the Gala?" Mike asked Ellie that evening.

She nodded.

"Good," he said. "You deserve to do really well, you've worked ever so hard this year."

Ellie grinned. She so wanted to win.

"My mum and dad are coming, and my grandmother who lives in Worthing, and my aunty who lives in Somerset. My mum's best friend and her daughter might come as well," Polly said, pushing Ellie out of the way with a bony elbow.

All that family! Ellie thought.

And all mine do is argue. Except this morning.

Ellie wanted her mum and dad to be happy like that all the time, and suddenly she made up her mind to do something about it.

She told Bert that evening.

"I've decided something," she whispered. "I'm going to tell Mum and Dad I don't like them shouting at each other. I'm going to tell Mum I'm fed up with tuna sandwiches as well."

GOOD ON YA, ELLIE, BUT DON'T THINK IT'S GOING TO BE EASY. TELL THEM ABOUT POLLY AS WELL IF SHE'S STILL BEING NASTY TO YOU.

That night, Ellie slept really
well and dreamed about
winning, and Mum (with stars
in her hair) and Dad (on a
unicycle) cheering her on.

Meanwhile,
two people Joseph was
in prison with had dreams and
he told them what they meant. The
cook was to die, the king's servant was
to be let out of prison. Both dreams came
true. Two years later the king of Egypt
dreamt he was standing beside the River Nile.
Seven fat cows started eating grass, then seven
ugly skinny cows came out of the river and ate
the fat ones.

The next morning the king was upset so he
called his wise men and told them what he
had dreamt. None of them could tell him
what the dreams meant.

Then the king's servant
remembered Joseph.

AT LAST. THE SERVANT'S SAID SOMETHING AND JOSEPH'S OUT
PRISON AND TELLING THE KING THERE'S GOING TO BE SEVEN
YEARS WITH LOTS OF FOOD FOLLOWED BY SEVEN YEARS WITH NO
FOOD. EVEN BETTER, JOSEPH'S BEEN PUT IN CHARGE OF LOOKING
AFTER ALL THE FOOD FROM THE GOOD YEARS SO THAT NO ONE
WILL GO HUNGRY IN THE BAD YEARS.

CHAPTER 5
THE GALA

The day of the Gala finally came.

"I think you're going to win!" Ellie told Toni once more as the girls' 100 metres freestyle was called.

"You reckon? I'll do my best!"

Toni straightened the straps of her new costume. Polly was next to her in black stripes, looking smooth and confident. Even her toenails were painted black.

"Go, Toni," Ellie breathed as they waited for the Klaxon hooter to start the race. Bad dive, Toni had gone too deep and when they surfaced, Polly was in front.

But Toni was coming back with every stroke.

The race was nearly over and Toni was putting in one last frantic effort.

The wall was nearly there.

"Go, Toni!"

She had done it!

And not only had she won, but she had swum fast enough to go through to the county finals.

"You're going to the finals! You're going to the finals!" Ellie chanted as Toni's towel settled beside her.

"I know! I know! I can't wait!"

And then Polly's shadow fell on them both, as she looked down with a face like thunder.

"You won because you did a false start. You dived in before the hooter went," she spat at Toni.

"She did not," Ellie said, standing up so her eyes were level with Polly's shoulders.

"She went the same as everyone else. Just because she's faster than you."

"Huh! Just wait until the county finals. I'm going as well. Then we'll see."

And with that Polly Hughes headed for the changing room.

Twenty minutes later it was Ellie's turn to wriggle her toes round the curve at the front edge of the starting box. She was determined to win.

"Take your marks." They bent over, ready to dive.

The Klaxon hooter blasted. They were off!

Ellie sensed Kristie in the next lane pulling slightly ahead of her.

On and on… she must do her very best… for Mum and Dad.

Maybe they'd stop shouting at each other if she won.

Maybe they'd be so proud of her they'd forget about Mum being a clown and…

Second.

That was all she had managed.

Even though she had swum the fastest she had ever swum in her whole life, Kristie had still beaten her.

"Hard luck," Toni said as Ellie returned to her seat. "You nearly won that as well."

"I know," Ellie sighed, then she grinned. "I was fast enough for the county finals though! Just!"

"That's brill!" Toni hugged her friend. "We can go together."

"Here's your mum and dad," Toni added.

"We were so proud of you," Mum said, giving Ellie a hug.

Dad ruffled her hair.

"Well done," he grinned, "and a whole second off your fastest time."

They were proud of her and she knew it, and Polly's parents and the coach load of people they had brought to cheer her on were nowhere to be seen. After all, second is not winning, and that was all they were interested in.

CHAPTER 6

THE ENVELOPE

The next four weeks flew by.

Polly took to doing fancy dives and showing off her new waterproof watch.

Everyone else used the clock on the wall. It was bigger and you didn't have to stop swimming to look at it.

At school they had lots of boring tests which Kevin missed because he had fallen out of a tree and broken his leg.

"He's always in trouble," his mother said when she came to school to collect some work for him.

Mrs Jenkins nodded.

That was the same day Ellie had asked Mum to stop giving her tuna sandwiches.

She had cheese ones instead.

"They might make your feet smell," Mum had said.

Joseph was 30 when the king made him governor. For seven years there were harvests of grain. Joseph collected and stored up the extra grain. There was so much grain they stopped keeping records.

Then the seven years of famine began and Joseph opened the storehouses and sold the grain. People from all over the world came to Egypt to buy it.

Mum and Dad didn't seem to be arguing as much either. Ellie was glad about that.

Maybe she wouldn't have to ask them to stop. Everything was just happy and normal.

JOSEPH'S WIFE HAD TWO SONS, AND ONE OF THEM WAS CALLED MANASSEH, WHICH MEANS 'GOD HAS LET ME FORGET ALL MY TROUBLES'. JOSEPH'S HAPPY LIKE ELLIE IS AT THE MOMENT, AND THAT'S NICE.

And then the envelope arrived.

It was addressed to Mum and inside was a letter.

The Clown Course was next month.

"I can't believe you're spending all that money," Dad groaned.

"Well, I am. It's something I have wanted to do all my life, and you're not going to stop me!"

Was now the time to tell Mum and Dad to stop shouting at each other?

Ellie opened her mouth, then closed it.

Dad was telling Mum he hated her hair (which was now yellow).

Ten of Joseph's brothers went to Egypt to buy grain and bowed their faces when they saw him. They did not recognise Joseph but he knew who they were. But he didn't let on who he was. The time wasn't right yet.

WELL DONE, NOW WAS NOT THE RIGHT TIME.

CHAPTER 7
ELLIE SAYS SOMETHING

The day of the county finals was brilliant for lots of reasons.

Toni not only beat Polly, once again, but also set a personal best time which was fast enough for her to go to the regional finals.

Polly was gutted and stormed off to the changing rooms in tears. This year, her swimming career ended at county level.

"I feel a little bit sorry for her," Toni said.

GIRLS

Inside, Ellie did too. Just a little bit.

Then Ellie knocked two whole seconds off her own best time.

She looked at Mum (now with bright orange hair) and Dad (dressed in his suit because he had come straight from work) who were sitting next to the milkshake machine.

Dad put his thumbs up. Mum waved and grinned.

Somehow it didn't matter that she had come fifth. She had done her very best.

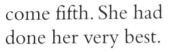

But the day got even better.

On the way home Mum mentioned the Clown Course.

"I'll be glad when that is over," Dad sighed.

Ellie took a deep breath.

"Will you stop shouting at each other then?"

She had said it, calmly, quietly, from the back of the van.

It was a moment before either Mum or Dad said anything.

Then Dad said, "We've had a lot going on lately. Has it worried you?"

Ellie didn't say anything. The seat belt was rough as she pressed it between her thumb and fingers.

"It has, hasn't it?" Mum was looking over her right shoulder.

Ellie nodded, a tear pricking the back of her eyes, running round, getting ready to roll down her cheek.

"I thought you were going to split up," she whispered.

"Ellie," Dad said, "your mum and I disagree about things and shout at each other sometimes, but that doesn't mean we're going to split up — even if I am married to a clown who pretends to be an orange daffodil."

"Oy! I'm not a clown yet."

"Well, you will be soon."

"And when I am, I'll teach you to juggle properly if you like," Mum offered.

And to Ellie's surprise, Dad laughed.

They went to Percy's Pizza Place on the way home.

Ellie had a Whopper Topper. So did Dad.

Mum had a salad. She was on a diet. Again.

"Bert," Ellie whispered, one evening, "everything is going to be OK."

YOU RECKON?

And Bert, as usual, just listened.

Eventually, Joseph told his brothers who he was.

"I am your brother Joseph," he told them, "the one you sold into Egypt. Don't worry or blame yourselves for what you did. God is the one who sent me ahead of you to save lives. Tell my father. Hurry and bring him here."

They all hugged each other. What a family reunion!

Stories don't always end happily. A lot about Joseph's life was hard, but it helped him learn something about God. He learned that God would always listen to his prayers and would look after him. Sometimes things happened and he didn't understand why, but he still trusted God.